A Family Like Mine

A Family Like Mine

Edited by Kate Agnew

Illustrated by Garry Parsons

EGMONT

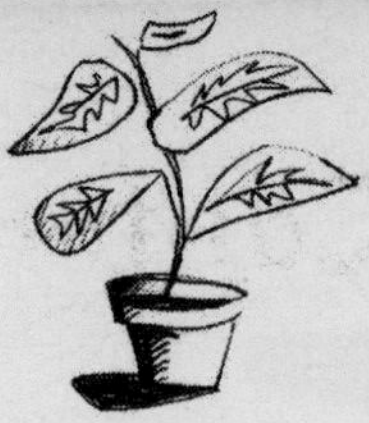

First published in Great Britain in 2003
by Egmont Books Ltd
239 Kensington High Street, London W8 6SA

ISBN 1 4052 0519 9

10 9 8 7 6 5 4 3 2 1

A CIP catalogue record for this title is available from the British Library

Typeset by Dorchester Typesetting Group Ltd
Printed and bound in Great Britain by Mackays of Chatham Ltd, Chatham, Kent

Contents

Introduction

What is it about families? Love them or loathe them, best friends or worst enemies, families stir strong emotions in all of us. Whether they cosset or cajole, praise or pressurise, whatever their idiosyncratic whims or irritating habits, they're unavoidably part of you.

And love them as you may, one of the things about families is that there's nearly always something about them you'd like to change. Maybe, like Emily in Francesca

Simon's story, *When I was a Girl*, you get fed up with your parents making comparisons between their childhood and your own. Or do you, like Tilly in Pippa Goodhart's story, *Tilly Dancing*, long to be just like your grandparents were? Perhaps – like Holly's dad in *The Great Xscape* – your dad is impossible once he's made his mind up about something. It could be that your family story is one of adventure, like the war-time tale Geoff Fox tells – a story based on something that really did happen to him in his own childhood.

There's always something fascinating about other people's families, something that makes them more interesting, more attractive, more exciting than your own. In Adèle Geras's tale, Marie, living just with her mum, doesn't want to write about her own home for the new teacher. Instead she invents a brand new family for herself, a family based on the large, cheerful household next door. Family life can bring both the greatest of fun and the strongest of emotions, and whatever the make-up of your own particular household, you hope your family will always be there for you when you need them. The children certainly need their mum's support in Rachel Anderson's delightfully comic *The Animals Came Out Two by Two*.

Whatever your own family, whether it's large or small, calm and peaceful or noisy and rumbustious, whether you get on well or fight at every opportunity, whether your family is the one you were born into, or one that's chosen you specially, whether it's just you and a grown-up, or whether you're part of a big sprawling family, there will be something in these stories to laugh at, to think about and to enjoy.

Kate Agnew

The Animals Came Out Two by Two

RACHEL ANDERSON

I always wanted a pet of my own. But my mum kept saying, 'No way!'

I said, 'Why not?'

She said, 'Because, Terri, as you well know, this cottage is too small.'

So I said, 'Oh *please*, Mum!'

And she said, 'What's wrong with the class gerbil at school?'

'I never get a turn looking after it.'

'That's probably because your teacher

doesn't trust you.'

Not many people did.

But then, one wonderful day, the old lady next door trusted me.

My little brother and I used to call her Miss Goats. Whenever we heard her going past, we ran over to the fence to listen. She made funny goaty noises.

'That's not kind, Terri. You know you shouldn't make fun of the poor old thing,' said Mum.

My big sister Tina agreed. 'You'll be an old lady yourself one day, Terri. You won't like it if you're teased just because you live alone and you never talk to anybody.'

Tommy, our little brother, said, 'My friend says she's a witch. That's why she won't speak.'

Mum said, 'Nonsense. She just likes to keep herself to herself.'

Tina said, 'And I don't blame her. So

would I if I had you two brats peeking through the fence at me.'

We all thought she lived on her own. We never saw anyone visit her cottage. We never saw her go anywhere, except down the lane with a bag collecting fresh grass, as if she thought it were something special to eat, until that day when we saw her coming round to call on us.

'What can she want?' said Mum.

Miss Goats had popping eyes and a wispy beard on her chin. Tommy got a fit of the giggles.

'She looks like a goat too!' he whispered.

Mum said, 'Do come in, Miss Gates.' (That was her real name.) 'Would you like a cup of tea?'

Miss Goats said, 'No. Can't stop now. I've come to ask a favour.'

'Why, of course,' said Mum, all smiles.

'I have to visit my sister. She's not well. I

wondered if one of your little ones would keep an eye on my little ones while I'm away?'

'Little ones?' I gulped. Miss Goats was much too old to have babies.

'Yes, dearie,' she said. 'Maud and her friends will need someone to give them their din-dins. And tuck them up for their beddy-byes.'

Maud was her cat. It was nearly as old as she was. It never came outside.

Mum looked doubtful.

But I quickly said, 'Ooh yes! I'll do it for you.'

'What a kind child. Young people are so helpful these days, aren't they?'

Mum gave me one of her special looks. 'Sometimes,' she muttered.

Miss Goats said, 'Here's the key then, dearie. And I'll leave a note for you on the table with the food. Remember to keep the

parlour door closed. Do you think you can manage?'

'Oh yes,' I said. I couldn't wait.

'And you will speak nicely to Maud, won't you? She gets so upset. Though I don't suppose the others will miss me.'

Later, we watched Miss Goats waiting in the lane for the bus. We saw her getting on with her luggage. We watched the bus leaving.

After tea, I said, 'Mum, I'm going round to Miss Goats' place now.'

Tommy wanted to come too.

'No,' I said. 'This is my job. It's too grown-up for you.'

Tommy said, 'Won't you be scared, going on your own?'

'Course not.'

But Miss Goats' garden was darker than ours. So I went back to get Tommy after all. I pretended I couldn't turn the key in

the lock. 'You might be able to do it better,' I said.

We went in together. There was nothing witchy about her cottage. It was the same as ours only the other way around.

If our cottage was too small for keeping pets, then so was hers.

Maud, the cat, was in the kitchen asleep on a broken armchair. The other pets were in the parlour.

'Wow!' I said. I was really pleased. 'I didn't know there were going to be this many!'

'Whew! What a pong!' said Tommy.

The room was a little bit smelly.

There were:

two guinea pigs in a pen on the floor
two blue budgies in a cage on a shelf
two green parrots in a cage on a stand
two fat goldfish and two tiny red fish
with floaty tails in a glass tank on
the dresser

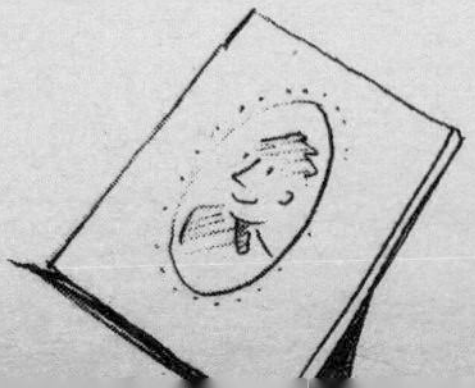

two terrapins in another tank

The third glass tank was full of green leaves. I couldn't see what was in there.

Miss Goats had left a note on the table, just like she said she would.

WELCOME TO OUR HOME
signed,
Maud, Smudge, Tickles, Spot,
Phoebe, Lawrence, Henry, Goldy,
Earl, Jacky, Blossom, Blanche,
Fluffkins, Sticky and Twiggy

The last two turned out to be stick insects in the tank with all the leaves. But I couldn't work out which the other ones were, apart from Maud.

I fed her first with food from the tin. She didn't take any notice, just blinked and went back to sleep. Then I went into the parlour to see the others. Some needed

Choco

clean water. Some needed fresh straw. It took quite a long time.

'Don't touch anything, Tommy!' I warned.

'I won't. Just looking.'

But of course he didn't *just look*. He climbed up onto a chair so he could see right into the goldfish tank.

'Poor things,' he said. 'They're ever so fed-up.'

I sent him outside to pick some grass for the guinea pigs. We gave them a carrot and some oats, too.

None of the creatures took any notice of their food. The guinea pigs shuffled back under their straw. The birds sat quietly on their perches. The stick insects kept so still you could hardly see they were there. The terrapins were as quiet as empty shells.

But all the creatures were looking at us. There were so many pair of eyes staring.

'It's sad,' said Tommy. 'They all look unhappy. They must be missing her.'

'Course they're not,' I said. 'They're just sleepy because it's their bedtime. Goodnight cat. Goodnight creatures!' I remembered to call out as we closed the back door.

'Everything OK?' Mum asked when we got home.

'Yes,' I said.

But next day I thought Tommy might be right because they all looked even sadder.

Tommy said, 'Perhaps we should do something for them.'

'What sort of something?'

'To cheer them up. If our mum went away and I was left shut indoors, I'd get miserable. Wouldn't you?'

He had an idea. He took a wooden spoon and he swished the water about in the goldfish tank. 'So it's like a big storm for them,' he said.

'Be careful,' I said, because I wasn't sure if it was a good idea.

But he was right. The fish did look happier swimming about in slurpy waves.

So we made some fun for the stick insects too. We took them out and let them walk up our arms.

'They're creepy,' I said. They were tickly too.

Next, Tommy lifted the guinea pigs from their pen. He put them on the floor. They didn't run about. They did some poos on the rug and they snuffled.

We took the terrapins out of their tank and put them on the mat to see if they'd like to talk to the guinea pigs. But the terrapins crawled away towards the shadows under the chairs.

None of the creatures were really enjoying playtime until Tommy decided it was time to let the birds out.

The Animals Came Out Two by Two

'Are you sure it's a good idea?' I said.

'Yes. It's horrible for them being shut in cages. They need free-fly time.'

So I checked all the windows to make sure they wouldn't fly right away into the open sky.

At first, they looked surprised. Then, one by one, they came out of their cages and sat on top. Then they flapped their wings and flew round the room. Tommy was right. They did seem to be having a very nice time.

Until suddenly, it all changed.

We'd forgotten about Maud in the kitchen. That sly cat was not asleep. She was awake. She was off her armchair. She was at the parlour door. She was nosing it open. She was in the parlour. She was ready for *her* playtime.

'Tommy!' I yelled. 'Watch out! The cat!'

Too late. Maud was everywhere. Pawing

at the guinea pigs on the floor. Sniffing out the terrapins under the chairs, flicking for the stick insects.

Then she took a flying leap for the birds. She missed. She hit one of the cages. It fell to the floor. Seed went everywhere. So did the little birds. They flapped this way and that round the ceiling. They flew back to the curtain rail and clung on tight. They were all cheeping loudly.

Maud did not give up. She leaped again. She pounced at the fish tank. She grabbed a goldfish. I tried to save it! But I was too late. Gulp. It had gone.

I got hold of her. 'You bad cat,' I said.

She was fighting hard. But I held on tight, then shoved her in the cupboard under the stairs. The rest of the creatures were going crazy and the birds wouldn't come down from the curtain rail. And Miss Goats' parlour was in a terrible mess, like a

whirlwind had been through it.

'We'll never sort this out,' I said. I was nearly crying. 'We need help. Fetch Mum!'

Mum was quite angry. 'What thoughtless children!' she said. But at least she knew how to catch birds. She got a teacloth and a saucepan lid.

Then she helped us clean up. Tina came and helped too. It took ages.

Tommy said, 'It looks tidier than before.'

Only one goldfish was missing.

Mum checked the cages were properly locked and the lids were on the glass tanks and grumpy Maud was back on her armchair.

Mum said, 'Tomorrow, I'll buy some more birdseed. And I'll see if I can find another goldfish.'

'Thanks, Mum,' I said. She was the best mum.

When Miss Goats got back, she brought

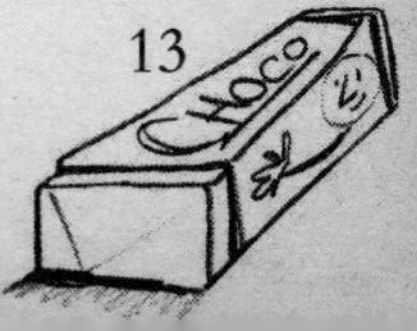

me a present. It was some fudge with a picture on the box of the seaside where her sister lived.

'Thank you, dearie,' she said. 'You've been most kind. I'm sure my little ones had a wonderful time. If I ever have to go away again, I'll know who to ask.'

'Thank you,' I said. But I knew I didn't deserve a present. I gave it to Tina.

Tommy said, 'I wonder if Miss Goats will notice that one of her goldfish is different?'

But if she has, she's never said anything. She's never been away again either.

Tilly Dancing

PIPPA GOODHART

I love dancing, don't you? When the music makes you move as if you're a puppet and your strings are pulling your arms and feet to the rhythm of the music's beat and the mood of the sound that surrounds you. Music makes stories in my mind so, when I dance, I'm acting too. My best kind of dancing is when I put on one of Gran's old dresses or a waistcoat or some ragged old skirt from the dressing-up box. Then I'm

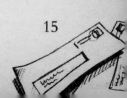

really part of the music's story. I dance a lot by myself in my bedroom. The only other person I really like to dance with is my grandad.

I've danced with Grandad since I was a baby. I can't remember much about being a baby, not nappies or anything like that, but I do remember dancing with Grandad. Sometimes there was jazzy music and Grandad would throw me up into the air where there was nothing to hold me, then I'd fall safe back into his big hands. Or there would be soft, swoopy, sleepy music. Grandad would hold me firm against his scratchy old jacket that smelt of earth and he'd rock me tick-tock to the music until I melted into sleep. I'm far too big for Grandad to pick up now, but we still dance. He's shown me how to do proper dances like the waltz – one, two, three, one, two, three – twirling slowly around his front

room. He's got music on old black records and a record player that scratches the sounds out of them. Waltzes are his best dance now. He's a bit too stiff for jazzy jiving and twisting. When he comes to our house, I put on a CD and play pop music. 'Just do whatever you feel like, Grandad,' I tell him. And he does for a minute or two. Then he sits and smiles and watches me.

'Just like your Granny Lil,' he'll say. Granny Lil was ill in hospital and could only walk a little with a walking stick, but she had been a ballet dancer. That was years ago, long before she had my mum.

One day, Grandad showed me pictures of young Granny Lil, and she was beautiful. There was an old cutting from a newspaper of her dressed all in white. Her arms were arching over her and her feet were pointing into the ground as if there was no bend at the ankles. Printed words

said 'Lillian Grace' under the picture. I could see that the person looking out of Lillian Grace's face was my Granny Lil. Grandad smiled at me and said, 'You should have heard the silence of a thousand people that held for a moment after Lil finished that dance, Tilly. And then they clapped two thousand hands together and cheered and threw flowers and I sat there so proud of her. So proud.'

That same night, Granny Lil died. When I saw Grandad next day his face was the way a balloon is when the air's mostly gone out of it, saggy and sad and old-looking. I hugged him. Then I told him, 'I'm going to be a ballet dancer like Granny.' Grandad patted my head with his great big hands.

I went to Miss Baker's classes in the school hall on Saturday mornings. I sat on the dusty floor and pulled on new, shiny,

real satin ballet shoes. I stood with the others and held onto the rail and stuck my feet out and pointed my toes. And when the music started, I curved an arm and scooped the air around me with the others. Miss Baker kept telling me, 'Bottom in, Tilly. Stomach in, feet out, head up.' All my bits seemed to be in the wrong place for her, but I felt right. I felt as if I was Lillian Grace with long loopy arms and head held high, almost flying like a bird as I skipped and jumped. The only thing I missed was having a story to dance, but then Miss Baker made an announcement.

'Girls, we are going to put on a show for your families and friends to come and see. We are going to dance the story of Cinderella.'

I told Grandad when he came to collect me. 'We're going to do Cinderella and you can come and see it like when you went to

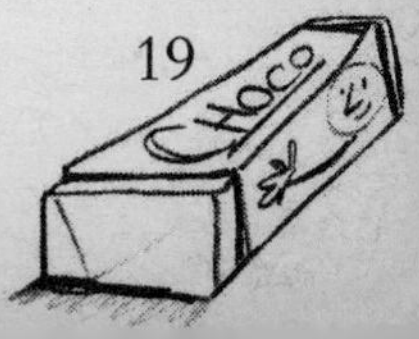

see Granny Lil.' I wanted him to be so proud of me.

All week I dreamed of what it would be like to be Cinderella. I went to my dressing-up box and found a ragged old skirt and a torn T-shirt for poor Cinderella, and practised sweeping floors, springing around with my toes pointed and a broom in my hand. Then I used one of Gran's old sparkling dresses to be beautiful Cinderella at the ball. I made the broom be the prince and went waltzing round and round. I knew I probably wouldn't be chosen to be Cinderella, but it was nice to dream, and Miss Baker had promised that we would be something.

But on Saturday morning there was a smell of sawdust and paint and something was different about the school hall. There was a long mirror all the way along one wall.

'Isn't it marvellous?' said Miss Baker. 'Now you'll be able to see what you look like and it will help us all improve our dancing.' And I saw what I'd looked like on the outside all that time when on the inside I felt like Lillian Grace. I saw a short, plump girl whose bottom and tummy stuck out when she jumped and whose feet never leapt as far as they should or pointed as much as they should. I looked at the tall, thin girls beside me, and at the girl in the mirror who was me, and I knew that I could only be picked to be the pumpkin or an ugly sister in the Cinderella show. I thought about that word; 'show'. I didn't want to show anybody else what the mirror had shown to me. I thought of Grandad and his lovely Lil, and I went to the side of the hall where the mirror couldn't see me. I took off my ballet shoes and I pulled my jumper over my leotard,

and I sat and waited for the end of the class.

'Don't you feel like dancing any more?' asked Miss Baker.

'No, I don't.'

'What's up?' asked Grandad as we walked home.

'I'm not going to dance any more,' I told him. Grandad stopped walking and looked at me.

'Why?' he asked. 'What about that show you were telling me about?'

'I'm not good enough.'

'Who says that? You're a lovely little dancer!'

'I look wrong. I don't look at all like Gran did. I look more like, like . . .'

'Like me?' said Grandad. And it was true. Grandad is a round sort of person too. Grandad held my hand. 'We can't all be

professional ballet dancers, Tilly. It'd be a funny old world if we were!'

'But I know how the dancing feels in my head! Why can't I do it on the outside?

'You keep trying and you'll learn to be a lovely dancer,' said Grandad.

'No,' said Tilly. 'I'm never going to dance again.'

'Not even with me?'

'Not even on my own.'

'So, should I never dance again either, just because I wouldn't make a handsome Prince Charming in a show?'

I shook Grandad's hand. 'Of course not!'

'Well then. You and I can go on enjoying our dancing as we always have done. We don't need other people to admire us.'

'But it must be so exciting being part of a show.'

'It must. It was wonderful for your gran when it all went well. But there were hard

times too – injuries and not getting parts she wanted as she got older and so on. I don't think it was as much fun as you and I have with our dancing.'

'But it must be lovely to be clapped. Has anybody ever clapped for you, Grandad?' Grandad thought for a moment.

'They did a few years back when I won a prize for my kind of show. And I didn't do any dancing to win it, you'll be glad to know!'

'What kind of show's that?'

'I'll show you,' he said.

Grandad led Tilly to his garden.

'Look,' he said. 'See that? Those poppies dancing in the breeze are my gypsy dancers, wild and bright. And the delicate hairbells, they're my fairies. And marigolds are firey suns.'

'What are those?' asked Tilly. She was crouched beside shaggy flowers in pinks and purples.

'Those are asters. What do you think they should be?'

'I think they look like big skirts dancing at a ball. They are the ladies at the ball Cinderella went to.'

'What about the men at the ball?'

'They should be bright, beautiful butterflies dancing with the lady flowers.'

'So where's Cinderella?'

'Oh, she's over there!' Tilly pointed to a white lily. 'Except that Cinderella would be in a dandelion dress, or something else that's a weed, in the early part of the story.'

'And the horrible stepmother is a red hot poker and the ugly sisters are cabbages!' Grandad snapped his fingers. 'I've got it!' he said. 'Tilly, love, you shall be part of the show. Why don't you see if Miss Baker needs help with the costumes? You know about dressing up and you're full of ideas.

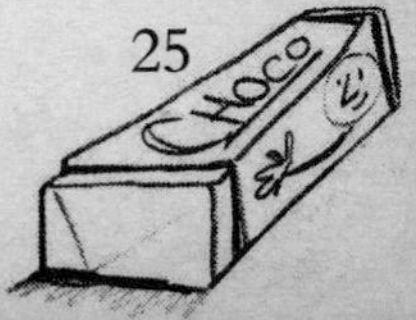

You'd be perfect for the job!'

So Grandad took me to see Miss Baker and she said, 'If you're quite sure that you don't want to dance, then we would love to have your help with the costumes, Tilly. Could you draw pictures of your lovely flower and butterfly ideas for us?'

So Grandad and I worked out what each of the characters in the story should wear, and I drew them. Then the sewing people made them almost exactly as I'd imagined them. They were beautiful. On show night, I was behind the curtains, helping the dancers get dressed and ready. It was scary and exciting, just doing that. I was really glad that the curtain wasn't going to pull back and show everyone me dancing.

Miss Baker took me with her to the back of the hall to watch the show. The hall went dark and the curtains went back and the lights shone on Cinderella in her dandelion dress, sweeping the hearth. I felt like the person who's coloured in a picture. It was nice feeling. There was the whole story, made the way I'd seen it in my head and shown to a whole audience. I could hear people whispering nice things about how it looked. I had my hands clutched tight the whole time it was going on.

When it ended, it was just the way Grandad had said. There was a moment when everyone was just still and quiet, and then there was shouting and clapping and I could see Grandad looking over his shoulder and clapping specially for me. Miss Baker made me go up onto the stage with her and bow with the dancers. I saw Grandad pull out his handkerchief and wipe his eyes, and when we walked home together he told me, 'I'm so proud of you, Tilly, so proud.' And I said, 'You know what

I feel like doing, Grandad?'

'What's that?'

'I feel like dancing!'

'So do I,' said Grandad, and we danced down the road together, and the funny thing was that I didn't care whether anybody else saw us or not.

When I was a Girl

FRANCESCA SIMON

The house looked like any other house.

'Look, Emily, that's where I lived when I was a girl,' said her mother.

'Most of these other houses weren't here then. Oh, there's the path where my sister and I used to ride our bikes.'

'Big deal,' muttered Emily. What did she care about some old house? Mum warbled on. 'Ellen and I had such fun here. We always got along so well – not like some

sisters I could mention.' Mum sneaked a look at Emily. Emily scowled.

'Come on,' said Mum. 'Let's see if there's still a tree house at the back. We can peek through the door in the garden wall. Just wait till you see the garden!'

'No,' said Emily. 'I don't want to.' Mum was always dragging her places she didn't want to go.

'Please,' said Mum. 'I'd really like you to see my old house.'

'No,' said Emily. She wanted to be home, playing computer games or riding her bike, not stuck here in the middle of nowhere looking at a boring old house.

'All right,' said Mum. She seemed a little sad. 'Then wait for me in the car. I'll be right back.'

Mum disappeared down the path. Emily scrunched down in the front seat and waited.

And waited.

Mum was taking forever, she thought crossly. Her legs felt stiff from sitting.

Emily got out of the car and stomped down the cracked concrete path.

'Mum!' she bellowed.

There was no answer.

'Mum!' she shouted again.

Still there was silence.

Then, faintly, Emily heard voices coming from the walled garden of Mum's old house. Mum must have gone in, got chatting, forgotten all about her. Typical, thought Emily. She turned the handle of the rickety wooden door cut into the wall and pushed it open.

Emily stared at the small, untidy garden, with its mossy lawn scattered with toys and bikes and an overgrown tree at the back. Strange it was so small, thought Emily, the way Mum talked about it you'd have

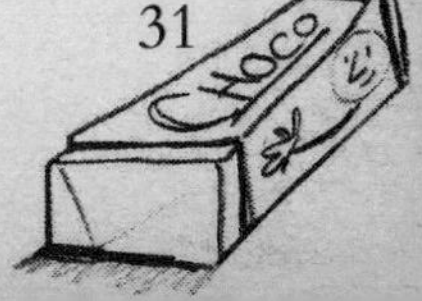

thought it was as big as Hyde Park.

A girl of about her age was sitting high up in a tree house. She stared down at Emily.

'What happened to your skirt?' she said, laughing.

Emily looked down at her leggings.

'I'm not wearing a skirt.'

The girl in the tree snorted.

'I can see that, numbskull. Where is it?'

'Nowhere,' snapped Emily. What a rude girl. 'I never wear skirts. I hate skirts. I'm wearing leggings, as you can see perfectly well.'

'What are leggings?'

Emily stared at the strange girl.

'What I'm wearing, of course. Everyone wears these.'

The girl smiled at her. 'Those are tights,' she said. 'You've forgotten to put your skirt on. I'd never go out dressed like that.

Everyone would laugh at me.'

Emily decided to change the subject.

'I'm looking for my mum.'

The girl swung along the branches.

'She's not here,' she said. 'What's your name?'

'Emily.'

The girl considered. 'Mine's Jessica. So where's your mum?'

'I don't know. I thought she was here. She lived in this house a long time ago.'

'Parents are always wandering off,' said Jessica. 'Come on up.'

Emily hesitated. She loved climbing trees but Mum always said it was too dangerous.

'Okay,' she said, and scrambled up the branches into the tree house. Mum would turn up sooner or later. Meanwhile, what she didn't know wouldn't hurt her.

The girls dangled their legs over the side.

'Hey, I like your shoes,' said Jessica. 'How do you keep them on without any laces?'

'Velcro,' said Emily.

'Vel-*what*?' said Jessica.

'Velcro,' said Emily. She ripped open her trainers, then closed them again.

'Wow,' said Jessica. 'I've never seen anything like that. And your watch. That's so neat. It doesn't have hands. Where did you get it?'

Emily looked at Jessica to see if she was teasing.

'It's just a plain old cheap digital watch,' said Emily.

'Do you come from far away or something?' said Jessica.

'No,' said Emily. 'London.'

'Oh,' said Jessica. 'London. I'd hate to live there.'

'Better than here,' said Emily.

'No it isn't,' said Jessica.

'Yes it is,' said Emily. 'It's boring here.'

'*I* like it,' said Jessica. 'I'm never leaving.'

At that moment a little girl dashed out of the house.

'Quick, hide,' hissed Jessica. 'That's my sister. Ignore her. She's a total brat.'

The girls flattened themselves on the tree house floor. But it was too late.

'Can I come up?' whined Jessica's sister.

'No!' said Jessica.

'Please?'

'No. Go away,' said Jessica.

The little girl looked round, then jumped on a red bicycle lying on the grass.

'Hey! Off my bike!' shrieked Jessica. 'Ellen! You little brat. I'm warning you! Get off it! Now!'

Ellen giggled and carried on riding.

Jessica scampered down the tree. There was a tearing sound as the pocket of her shorts caught on a branch.

Jessica ran after Ellen, pulling her off the bike.

Ellen screamed and slapped Jessica.

Jessica slapped her back. Ellen burst into tears.

'Mum! Carol slapped me!'

'Mum!' screamed Jessica. 'Ellen slapped me first.'

A woman poked her head out of the upstairs window.

'Stop squabbling, girls!' she shouted. 'Can't you play together for five minutes without fighting? Ellen! Ride your own bike. Carol, what's happened to your shorts?'

'Sorry, Mum,' said Jessica.

'Please try to be more careful,' said her mother. 'I'm sure I took better care of my clothes when I was a girl. Who's your friend?'

'I'm Emily,' said Emily. 'I'm waiting for my mum.'

'If she doesn't come soon you're very welcome to stay for a snack.'

Emily stared at Jessica's mother. She reminded Emily of someone, but Emily could not think who.

'Why'd she call you Carol?'

'Because that's my real name,' said Jessica. 'I hate it. I'm trying out lots of new names to find one I like better. This week I'm Jessica.'

'Carol's my mum's name,' said Emily. 'She hates it, too.'

'I'm not surprised,' said Jessica.

'Your mum's nice,' said Emily.

Jessica made a face.

'She's always picking on me,' she said.

'So is mine,' said Emily. 'She's always telling me how perfect she was when she was a girl.'

'My mum does that too,' said Jessica. 'It's so annoying.'

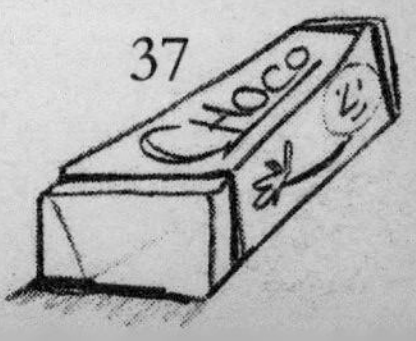

'I can tell you one thing, I won't pick on my children,' said Emily.

'Me neither,' said Jessica. 'But I'm not having children. Too much trouble. When I grow up I'm going to be an astronaut. Look,' she pointed, 'you can see the moon now.'

The girls looked up at the late afternoon sky.

'Do you think someone will ever walk on the moon?' said Jessica.

'Of course I do, 'cause lots of people already have,' said Emily. 'Where have you *been*?' Jessica didn't seem dumb, but she sure said dumb things sometimes.

Jessica frowned. She liked Emily, but she sure said dumb things sometimes.

'If you don't believe me, you can ask my mum,' said Jessica. 'Mum!' she bellowed. 'Mum!'

'What is it?' shouted Jessica's mother.

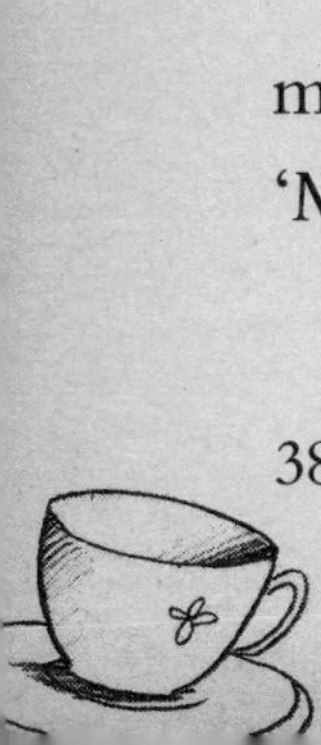

'Has anyone ever walked on the moon?'

Jessica's mother stuck her head out the window.

'I'm trying to get supper ready, Carol. Don't ask silly questions.'

'Well have they?' asked Jessica.

'Of course not,' said Jessica's mum.

'Told you,' said Jessica.

'People *have* walked on the moon,' said Emily. 'They have. I know they have.'

'I think I'd know about it if they had,' said Jessica.

'Not necessarily,' said Emily.

'What's that supposed to mean?' demanded Jessica.

'Uh, maybe people who live here learn a different history,' said Emily, lamely. She really liked Jessica; why did they start squabbling so easily?

'Biscuits are on the table,' called Jessica's mum.

Ellen dropped her bike and raced inside.

'C'mon, let's go in before the pig eats them all,' said Jessica.

Emily followed her into the house, then stopped in the sitting-room and stared. A big, old-fashioned black and white TV stood blinking in the corner.

'I bet you've never seen one of these before,' said Jessica.

'Not in real life,' said Emily. 'Is it an antique?'

'No, it's a television,' said Jessica. 'We just bought it. We're the first people I know who have one.'

Emily opened her mouth to say something, and then closed it. She didn't want to be rude and brag about her video and colour TV. Poor Jessica, thought Emily. She never knew life was so different outside London.

The girls sat down at the table. Jessica's

mother handed round biscuits and milk.

'You know what,' said Emily, 'you look a bit like my grandma.'

Jessica's mother frowned.

'Oh,' she said. She put her hand up and touched her dark hair. 'Do I look that old?'

'I don't mean how she looks now,' said Emily, quickly. 'When she was younger. A lot younger.'

'Oh,' said Jessica's mum again. 'I see. When is your mother coming?'

'I don't know,' said Emily. 'She used to live here.'

'When was that?' said Jessica's mum.

'A long, long time ago,' said Emily. 'When she was a girl.'

I wonder what she was like then, thought Emily suddenly. It was so hard to imagine Mum ever being young. And where was Mum, anyway?

Then faintly, Emily heard her mother's

voice floating towards her, calling her name as if from far, far away.

Emily jumped up.

'I hear Mum,' she said. 'I must go. Thank you for the biscuits. Bye, Jessica!'

Emily ran into the garden. Jessica followed.

'I'm coming, Mum!' she shouted. She ran over to the door in the wall, and tripped over the hose.

'Owwwww!' yelped Emily.

Blood dripped from a cut on her hand.

'I'll get you a plaster,' said Jessica.

'No,' said Emily. 'Mum's calling.'

Jessica reached into her pocket and pulled out a bright, yellow, polka dot handkerchief. The edges were embroidered, rather sloppily, in blue and red thread.

'Use this then,' she said, wrapping it round Emily's hand. 'I sewed it myself.'

'Thanks,' said Emily. 'Do you think we'll

ever see each other again?'

'I hope so,' said Jessica. 'I like you.'

'I like you, too,' said Emily.

And she walked through the door.

Mum was coming up the path.

Emily ran to meet her.

'Oh, Emily, you've torn your leggings,' said Mum.

'Sorry,' said Emily.

'Please try to be more careful,' said Mum. 'I'm sure I took better care of my clothes when I was a girl.'

'What took you so long?' said Emily.

'I was just gone for a few minutes,' said Mum. 'I've been looking everywhere for you. Where have you been?'

'In your old garden,' said Emily. 'It was wonderful. You never told me.'

Mum smiled. 'How'd you get in?'

'Through the door,' said Emily. 'Just like you said.'

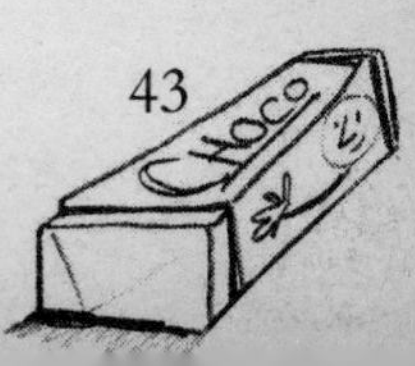

'It's not there anymore,' said Mum. 'I looked.'

'Well, I found it,' said Emily. 'I'll show you.'

She marched back down the path, then stopped. She remembered the path being shaded by high hedges. Now they were all neatly trimmed. She kept walking beside the garden wall, looking and looking for the door.

'You've gone too far, Emily,' said Mum.

'But there was a door,' said Emily. 'I went in. I played with a girl called Jessica. She even had a sister called Ellen, just like you do.'

'Perhaps you imagined it,' said Mum.

'I didn't,' said Emily. 'I didn't. Jessica!' she screamed. 'Jessica!' There was no answer.

'Maybe it was a different house,' said Mum.

'No,' said Emily. 'It was right here.'

Mum smiled. 'That's very strange.'

Then she stopped smiling. 'What's happened to your hand?'

'I fell. Jessica gave me her hankie to stop the blood.'

Mum took Emily's hand and looked at the handkerchief.

'That's funny,' she said. 'That looks just like a hankie I had when I was a girl.'

The Borrowdales

ADÈLE GERAS

Marie nibbled a little row of toothmarks into the top of her pencil and stared at the title she'd written down in her exercise book. 'MY FAMILY,' it said, in her very neatest writing. She'd underlined the words with a ruler. She'd put a date in the margin. She was ready to start her homework, but she had a problem. It wasn't a problem she could do very much about, and most of the time she dealt with it quite well, but this homework was exactly the thing, the one thing in the whole world she didn't want to write about, for the simple reason that she didn't have a family – not even the slightest bit of one.

There was her (Marie Evans) and there was her mum (Nesta Evans) and that was that. Her mother was an only child and an orphan. Both of Nesta's parents had been only children. Her husband, Marie's dad, was also parentless, brother – and sisterless and the only child of only children. It was one of the things, Marie's mum always said, that had brought them together in the first place. Unfortunately, Marie's father had died when she was two, so she couldn't write very much about him either.

She sucked at the pencil's chewed-up end. This was the very first piece of homework she'd been given in her new school. Marie and her mum had just moved into a new house and she hadn't even had time to make any friends. No one knows me, she thought. No one knows anything at all about me. And suddenly an idea flashed into her mind. It was such a brilliant idea that she felt like a cartoon character with a lightbulb winking and blinking above her head.

The house next door was packed as full as any house could possibly be. Marie and her mum hadn't met them, because the family's house wasn't part of the estate at all, but left over from a time when there were fields all around. It was a big house: square and solid with ivy growing up the red-brick walls, and it kept itself to itself behind tall hedges.

Marie had a good view of the back garden from her bedroom window and because they'd moved in over the summer holidays, she'd had lots of opportunities to

watch the Martins. She knew their family name because the milkman had once talked about them to her mother, but all their first names were her idea. There was Granny Martin, who was chubby and wore her white hair in a rolled-up plait on top of her head. She was married to Grandpa Martin, who was red-faced and had no hair at all. He walked with a stick.

Mum Martin wore flowery skirts and brightly coloured T-shirts and dangly earrings and her hair was short and curly. Her name, Marie decided, was probably Patsy. She wore glasses with tortoiseshell frames and it was her voice Marie heard most often from the garden, especially her tinkly laugh.

Dad Martin (Graham, perhaps) was tall and skinny and dark. He went out every morning carrying a briefcase. The children were noisy and cheerful and there were

four of them, all older than Marie. Two boys and two girls. They kept coming and going in and out of the house, often surrounded by groups of friends. Marie called the boys Sporty and Scary and her names for the girls were Posh and Baby. Living next door to the Martins was like having a soap opera going on under your nose.

No one will know, Marie thought. I'll give them another name. I'll call them the Borrowdales because I'm borrowing them. She picked up her pencil and started to write.

'I live in my house with my mum. My dad died when I was two but I've got lots of relations. I've got a grandma and a grandpa. They're my mum's parents and they live in Wales. They are called the Borrowdales.'

Marie was pleased with that bit because it was *almost* true. Her mum had been born in Wales.

'They live in a big house. It has ivy growing on the walls. My uncle and aunt live there too. Their names are Graham and Patsy Borrowdale. I call them Uncle Graham and Auntie Patsy. They have four children.'

Marie had to stop and work out names and ages in her head.

'My cousins are David (16), Peter (14), Susie (13) and Megan (11). I like Susie and David best. Susie wears beautiful clothes and she's allowed to wear shoes with heels for special occasions, as long as they're not too high. She wears lipstick for parties.

'In their house there is always a lot of chat. Lots of friends come to visit.'

Marie stopped writing and gave the middle of her pencil a bit of a chew. The top was getting too soggy and splintery now. She decided to bring her homework to an end before she got carried away, and wrote:

'I like my family very much. I wish they lived nearer to our house so we could see them more often. We always spend Christmas with them and I can't wait. I always get lots of presents. THE END.'

Marie drew a little sketch of Mrs Martin – *Borrowdale* – just as decoration. She coloured it in carefully and closed her exercise book. Writing about Christmas had made her feel sad. In the old house they used to share dinner with the Saunderses who lived across the road, but they didn't know anyone here well enough. She hoped that by December they might have met some people who had a lit-up tree in their front room and who liked turkey and roast potatoes and didn't mind wearing silly hats while they ate it.

Mrs Entwhistle, Marie's teacher, took ages to mark the homework. At the end of the week, Marie asked her about it.

'Don't worry, dear,' said Mrs Entwhistle. 'You'll have it back on Monday morning. I thought your piece was most interesting.'

Marie had to be satisfied with that. She decided to enjoy the weekend and not worry about her homework at all.

'Marie? Marie, are you up there?'

'What's the matter, Mum? I'm busy . . .' Marie had set up an elaborate game with her Barbie dolls and didn't feel like going all the way downstairs. It was Sunday afternoon, and there wasn't anything on TV for ages yet.

'There's someone here to see you . . .'

Marie ran downstairs. The front door

was open and there was Mrs Entwhistle. She wasn't alone, either. Standing next to her were Posh and Baby from next door. What were they all doing there?

'Hello, Marie,' said Mrs Entwhistle. 'I'd like you to meet my nieces, Josie and Freya.'

'Your nieces?' Marie blushed. She was confused. How could her next-door neighbours be related to her teacher?'

'My sister is your Mrs Borrowdale. What you wrote about the family rang a bell and your picture looked exactly like Eve, so I checked your address.'

Marie hung her head. 'I'm sorry,' she whispered. 'I made it all up. Only I didn't want to say I didn't have one. A family, I mean.'

'That's quite all right, dear,' said Mrs Entwhistle. 'Freya, you've got something to say, haven't you?'

Freya stepped forward and blushed. Marie realised that she must be feeling embarrassed too. Then Freya said, 'We've got a computer at our house. Do you like computer games?'

'I don't know,' said Marie. 'I've not played them much.'

'Come and try, then,' said Freya. 'You can stay for tea.'

'Thank you,' said Marie. She turned to Mrs Entwhistle and said again, 'I'm really sorry.'

Mrs Entwhistle leaned very close to Marie's ear and whispered, 'They have a huge tree at Christmas and they love playing dressing-up games. You couldn't wish for a better family to live next door to. Go on, then. Off you go and play some computer games. I'll just stay and have a word with your mum.'

Marie followed Freya and Josie down

the path. What would she talk to them about? she wondered. Fortunately Freya started speaking almost before Marie's front door had shut behind them.

'Have you really got no family?'

Marie nodded. Josie said, 'You can have our brothers with pleasure. We're sick to death of them.' She added. 'You can help us shove them off that computer. They hog it all the time.'

They all went through the gate together and into the front garden.

The Spitfire, the Fun Book, Grandpa and Me

GEOFF FOX

It's not easy to imagine your grandpa in short trousers, is it? It's a bit like trying to imagine your mum when she was a teenager going to wild parties. My mum says she sang in a girls' band and they nearly went professional, but I don't know whether to believe her. I'll get back to Grandpa's short trousers in a minute.

Nowadays, my grandpa grumbles a lot. He tries not to, but he can't really help it

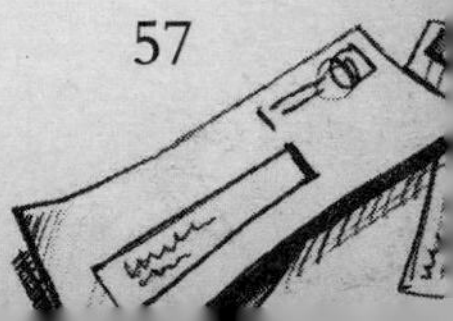

because he's got a lot to grumble about. I know why he grumbles, but knowing why doesn't always help when he's living with you seven days a week. He could do with a new hip for a start. He'd sleep better at nights and we could go for long walks the way we used to do. And he does miss Grandma. Sometimes I can hear Grandpa when he's in his bedroom (it's next door to mine) and he talks to Grandma as if she's still alive. I've even heard him crying, though he never does anything like that when Mum and I are around.

Right, let's get back to the short trousers. It was a few weeks after Christmas last year, and we'd just had Sunday lunch. I usually go out to play football in the park on Sunday afternoons, but the rain was belting down so we were sitting together in the lounge. I didn't feel like going on the computer so I picked up an old *Beano*

Annual and stretched out on the floor to read it again. Mum and Grandpa were having a cup of tea – they're always having cups of tea. Suddenly Grandpa chuckled.

'This is exactly how it was that afternoon. History repeating itself.'

'What do you mean?' Mum asked.

'It's just how it was when . . .' He stopped and looked at me for a moment. 'When I lost my *Knockout Fun Book for 1945*.'

Now you can always tell with Grandpa when there's a story coming on. He doesn't tell them very often but usually they're worth waiting for.

'David, nip upstairs into my bedroom, would you? In the bookcase opposite the door, bottom shelf, left-hand end, you'll find a whole row of *Knockout* annuals. Find the one for 1945 – it's the one with a picture on the cover of two lads with

fishing rods riding a donkey backwards being chased by Billy Bunter.'

I'm not usually allowed into Grandpa's room and I'm certainly not allowed to read his books unless he's there. You see, he collects old books and one or two of them are worth thousands of pounds. Well, I found the one he meant. There it was – *The Knockout Fun Book for 1945.* I looked inside it before I went downstairs again. There were lots of strip cartoons, jokes, and long stories about pirates, detectives and fighter-pilots and that sort of thing. It looked really good. I took it downstairs and gave it to Grandpa.

'I thought you said you'd lost it, Gramps.'

'So I did. I bought this copy in a second-hand bookshop only about ten years ago. Cost me a bob or two. Your grandma thought I was mad. Said it was time I grew up.'

'So what's the story then, Dad?' asked Mum. Later on, thinking about it, I realised Mum must have heard the story before, but she just wanted to get Grandpa to tell it to me. Grandpa looked through the book for a while, and then he started.

'It was a Sunday afternoon in wintertime, just like today, except it wasn't raining. Just after two o'clock and we'd had roast lamb for lunch – my favourite. Still is.'

I'd better tell you that Grandpa's stories are always like this. Loads of little details you think aren't important, but I like them. That's why I can remember them ages after he's told them. What I'm going to tell you is pretty much how he told the story to us (and I haven't forgotten the short trousers).

'It was 1945 and the war hadn't ended yet. I was nearly seven and my brother, Ernie, had gone off on the bus to Sunday

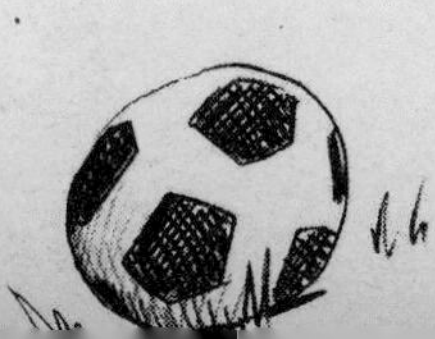

School about three miles away. He probably had the worst experience of all of us.

'Well, I was stretched out on the settee in our back room reading *The Knockout Fun Book for 1945,* which my Auntie Winifred had given me for Christmas. I'd probably read it twenty times already. Mum and Dad had been having a cup of tea, and what's more, they were using the same set of cups and saucers we're using now. And that's a bit of a miracle too, when you think about it.

'My dad had gone to sleep in his armchair. He was snoring away like an old steam engine, the way he usually did. My mum wouldn't let me nudge him or anything, though it really used to annoy me when I was trying to read.

' "Your father's dog-tired," she'd say. "Leave him be."

'And he was, because he usually worked seven days a week on the boats down at the docks, repairing the engines and getting them ready to go out to sea again. These were boats bringing food to Britain from America to keep us going during the war – and sometimes they'd been attacked by U-boats or bombed out on the Atlantic.

'Well, that particular Sunday he'd had a day off and he'd spent the morning in the garden. I'd helped him clean out the hens for a bit – we kept hens at the bottom of our garden during the war, because you couldn't buy enough eggs on your ration cards and my mum believed every day should start with an egg for breakfast. Dad had still got his Home Guard boots on because he used them for working in the garden. It was a good job he had, as it turned out.

'Mum was reading the *Sunday Express*

and I reckoned it wouldn't be long before she was asleep too. Then it happened.

'I was deep inside my annual when I heard an aeroplane engine. Not a jet plane – they'd hardly been invented, and I didn't see one of those until the war was over. But I knew about planes. I'd seen the German bombers going over when we were on our way to the air-raid shelter, and I'd seen the whole sky lit up a fiery red over the city more than ten miles away. They bombed the docks several times; Mum must have been really worried about Dad, working down there. I was too young to understand – whenever the air-raid sirens went I did what I was told, put on my Mickey Mouse gas mask and went into the shelter. Honestly, David, I'm not kidding you. They made gas masks with Mickey Mouse faces so that children would think an air-raid was some kind of dressing-up game.

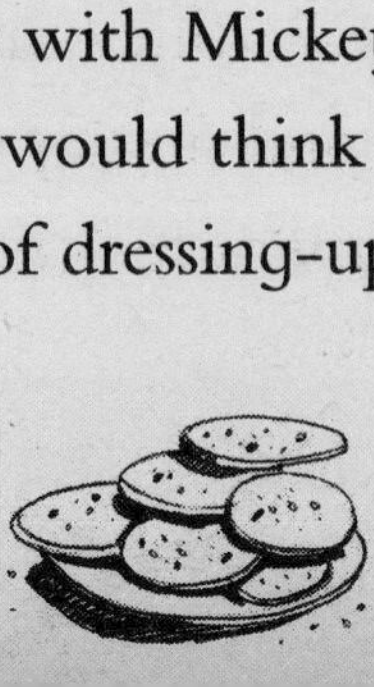

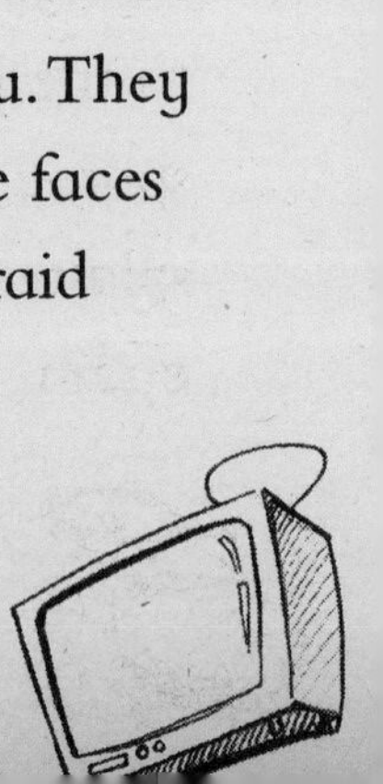

'This engine was different, though. The plane seemed to be much lower and even though I was still only six, I knew what that could mean. A Flying Bomb! The deadly Doodlebug – one of Hitler's latest inventions – a bomb with wings, but no pilot. They were a kind of rocket, you see. What you had to listen out for was when their engines cut out. That mean they were on the way down. One of them had dropped on a house in the next street to ours just before Christmas. Ernie and I had been round to have a look, though we weren't supposed to. There was just a hole where the house had been.

'Well, suddenly, the engine did cut out. I thought we'd had it. I jumped up and ran to the French windows to see if I could spot it. Then the engine coughed and spluttered a bit and finally started up again. Maybe it was me racing about or maybe he'd heard the engine too, but my dad woke up and came to look with me. There it was! Coming low over the trees along Riddings Road.

'It was a Spitfire. You could even see the red, white and blue roundels on the fuselage and the wings to show it was of ours.

'"Eh, David, if he comes down any lower, we'd better ask him in for a cup of tea, hadn't we?" Dad said. I think he could see I was worried and he just wanted to try to make me grin a bit. We could even see the pilot. He'd pushed the roof of the cockpit back and he seemed to be waving at people in their gardens down below. Later, I realised what he was trying to do.

'Then the plane passed out of sight over our row of houses and I went back to the settee. All of a sudden there was a huge roaring sound. Imagine you're on a railway

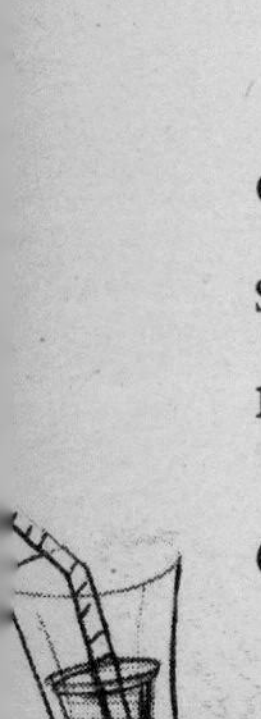

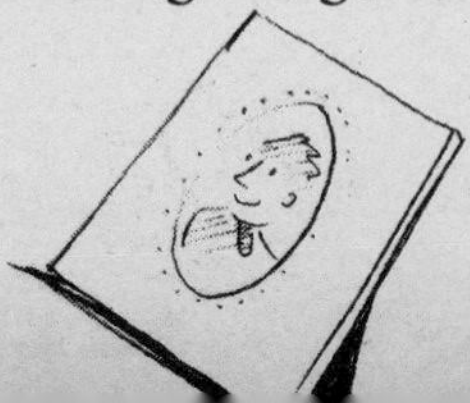

platform when one of those InterCity trains comes in – only it doesn't stop but flashes right past your nose. Imagine the noise of that, then multiply it by about ten, and that'll give you some idea. Like being in the middle of one of those tornadoes or whirlwinds, maybe – the kind they have in America.

'The whole house sort of trembled – as though it was shivering and couldn't stop.

'"Get on the floor, David!" my mum shouted and I rolled off the settee onto the carpet. And then there was an almighty THUMP and the wall between our lounge and the front room just blew apart. Bricks came flying across the room like a flock of pigeons.

'Mum threw himself down on the floor too, half-covering me with her body. Her armchair disappeared beneath dust and bricks and rubble. Dad was at the French

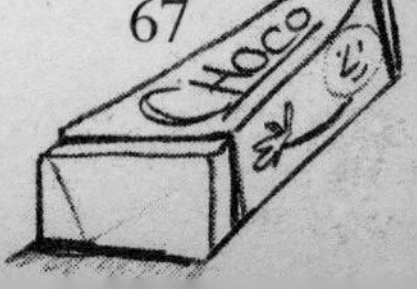

windows. I'd never seen those windows open in my life. They were more like doors than windows, really – mostly wood with glass in the top half. I think the lock needed sorting out and Dad had been too busy with all his war work on the boats to fix it. But he was a strong man, my dad. He'd been a bit of a boxer when he was younger – an amateur, you know, not a professional. He just balanced himself, lifted his right leg and kicked those doors through – which is why it was good he hadn't taken his Home Guard boots off.

'"Come on, quick," he yelled. Mum and I scrambled on all fours to the French windows and the three of us went racing down the garden.

'Not one scratch between us. That was the biggest miracle. Not a single scratch.

'We just stood there and Mum hugged us both. After a minute or two, Dad picked me up and sat me high on his shoulders just like when I was a baby. He carried me at a run round the side of the house and the first thing we saw was what was left of his car. A Hillman it was. FJA 774. Cut clean in two. The plane had crashed into the front of our house, and the wing had sliced through the car. What happened, according to Mr Russell who had been out in his garden next door, was that the wing tip of the Spitfire hit one of the old elm trees on our road. The plane spun right round and nose-dived straight into the front of our house. All the time, Mr Russell said, the pilot was waving to tell people on the ground to get out of the way. He must have had a cool head too, because he switched his engine off. Mr Russell said you could even hear him shouting before the plane hit the tree.

'We got past the car and there were

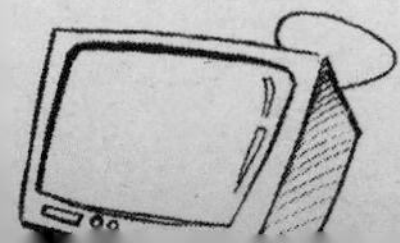

dozens of people running all over our front garden. Sticking up out of a tangle of wreckage was a great metal cross – the tail of the aircraft. The rest of the plane was buried in our front room. And the bedroom above had just dropped down on top of everything. That was the bedroom where my brother and I slept and I could see our beds had slipped down on top of the wreckage.

'I'll tell you something daft, David. I felt really embarrassed. Because round the bedroom wall for everyone to see was a wallpaper frieze. Cinderella, Little Red Riding Hood, teddy bears, a toy train, that sort of thing. All my friends would see it. It was baby stuff, and I was almost seven!

'Dad suddenly hoicked me down off his shoulders and gave me to Mum. He was off, climbing into the wreckage with lots of other men, trying to find the pilot somewhere in all that debris. You could see them throwing bricks and bits of broken furniture out of the way, digging to try to reach him with their bare hands. You know I said it was wintertime? Well there were two fires lit in our house that afternoon, one in the kitchen and one in the lounge. Hardly anyone had central heating in those days. Lots of the rescuers were smoking when they went looking for the pilot, you know, even though the whole place was drenched in aircraft fuel. Dad told me that all the experts said later that the plane should have exploded, what with the fires and everyone smoking. But it didn't. You know, the front room carpet which that Spitfire nose-dived onto was soaked in fuel too – but once they'd cleaned it, that carpet was fine. Not a hole in it. We used it for years. And these teacups we're drinking out of now – not one got

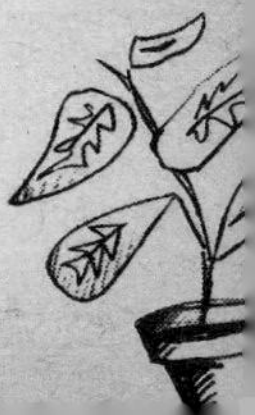

broken. But I did lose my *Knockout Fun Book*. It must have been buried under the bricks.

'And here's the sad bit, David. They don't always put this kind of thing in stories about wars. Just behind the dining-room door, they found the pilot. He was dead – probably before he hit the ground. When the plane caught the tree and spun right round, his neck would have snapped, they said. Dad was told the pilot had been flying up to Scotland to see his wife and their new baby – the poor chap never saw his own daughter.

'I was taken off to a neighbour's and she gave me a whole pile of comics to read. She even gave them to us to take away later that afternoon when we went to stay with my grandparents while our house was rebuilt. It took them almost a year. After we went back to live there, for ages we used to find bits of the plane buried in the flower-beds.'

'Go on, Dad,' said my mum. 'Tell him the bit about what was going on in the garage.'

'Are you sure? All right, I suppose it's part of the story. About half-an-hour after the crash, my dad went round the side of the house to our garage. He was a bit of a carpenter and he kept all sorts of things in there, including some fine tools – you know, saws, and planes and chisels. There was lots of good wood in there he'd saved from before the war and old clothes too, which Mum thought might come in handy for someone – you never threw anything away during the war. He loved those tools – I've still got two or three of them. There wasn't any room for the car in there, it was so full of things they were saving in case they came in useful.

'Dad saw the door was open a crack, so

he looked in. There was a chap in there he'd never seen in his life. This fellow had a couple of sacks, and he was loading them up with Dad's tools, pairs of shoes, clothing, anything of value. He was looting. People did that in the war sometimes when houses had been bombed.'

'What did your dad do?' I asked.

'I never found out. He wouldn't ever tell me. But he'd been a boxer, as I told you before. I don't suppose the man with the sacks stayed around very long.'

'And why did you say your brother Ernie had the worst of it? He wasn't even there.'

'No, but you see on the bus on his way home, everyone was talking about a plane that had come down. So he thought – right, I'll get my bike out and see if I can collect some bits off that plane. Lots of boys did that in the war. But when he got near our house, he could see all the fire engines and police cars and an ambulance and hundreds of people milling about. Well, you can guess what he thought. He thought there'd be no Mum, no Dad, and no me. If you'd seen that house you wouldn't have believed anyone could have got out alive.'

'So what did he do?'

'He ran as fast as he could towards the house and I wouldn't mind betting he started crying a bit. You would, wouldn't you? But before he got there, Mum came running towards him out of the crowd – she'd been watching out for him, you see. And she just put her arms round him and held him tight.

'All she said was, "It's all right, Ernest. We're all safe and sound, all four of us. That's all that matters."'

So that was Grandpa's story, just as he told

it to me. When he'd finished, he gave me the copy of *The Knockout Fun Book* to look at. That's where the short trousers come in.

As he passed it to me, a black-and-white photograph fell out. Well, more brown than black-and-white. Sepia, I think they call it. Old-fashioned. Quite large, it was. The kind people used to have done in a photographer's studio when Grandpa was a child. There was this little boy, sitting on a sort of bench. His hair is all neatly combed, he's got a school tie on, and he's wearing a neat pair of short trousers. You can tell he's not used to sitting still, though. He looks as if he can't wait to jump off that bench. He's about five or six, I think, and he's looking straight at you, smiling with his mouth open just a little bit, as though he's just going to say something.

I've got him framed up on my bedroom wall now. And when I hear Gramps snoring

on the other side of the wall, or even crying a bit, I take a good long look at that photograph.

The Great Xscape

LINDA NEWBERY

'Do you really mean to say,' Holly demanded, 'that we can't have Christmas *at all*?'

'No! Weren't you listening?' Dad was frowning at the television. Every channel was contaminated – a jingly tune with sleigh bells, a carol concert, a jolly quiz, adverts, adverts, adverts.

'Your father is a Christmas-refuser,' Mum explained. 'A Christmas-objector. A

Christmas-critic. I blame your grandparents – they shouldn't have christened him Noel. It's put him off for life.'

Holly giggled. She was used to Dad being Noel, but it must be weird having a name that meant Christmas. And who had Dad married? Mum – whose name was Carol.

Dad turned off the TV and tried the radio instead.

'I accuse you,' Jonny told him, 'of being a mean old Scrooge.'

'A Scroogey old meanie,' Holly added.

Dad glared at them. 'I am *not* mean. *Or* a Scrooge. *Or* old. I've told you, we'll have Christmas at the proper time. That's the way it used to be – nowadays it's all about spending and panic. Chrismania, that's what it is. I refuse to have two whole months of glitter and tat and *ho-ho-ho*ing.'

Christmas was banned from the house. The twins got it at school, of course – carols, a party, a pantomime. Mum smuggled mince pies into their bags for the party, but the rule at home was Christmas-Free Zone. No tree, no decorations, no cards. Holly made a defiant display of Christmas cards in her bedroom, and arranged wrapped presents on her desk. Just in case Dad should come in and be upset, she put a *Strictly Private – Keep Out* notice on the door. She resisted the urge to decorate it with robins or snowflakes, but if Dad had been in a prickly mood he might have argued about the very small holly leaf she drew in one corner. Still, Holly was her name, and who was to blame for that?

Jonny's small act of rebellion was to exclaim, 'Ho *ho*!' in Dad's hearing, just stopping short of the third *ho*, whenever there was a shower of cards through the

letter box. Anything suspiciously Christmassy had to be snatched off the doormat and put into a bin-liner Mum was hiding in a cupboard.

Dad had planned the Great Xscape ages ago, back in the summer, when – even before the school holidays were quite over – gift catalogues sneaked themselves into the house. Bundling them into the recycling bin, Dad retreated into the newspaper, where he found, in the small print, an advert for a holiday cottage in the Peak District, miles from anywhere. Immediately he started making plans and telephone calls.

'We'll be away from everyone except ourselves,' he explained. 'Our Christmas will start on Christmas Eve, not before.'

When it was time to leave, everything was packed into bin-liners, even the Christmas tree. The family might have been

setting off for the rubbish tip. There wasn't a glint of glitter to be seen: not a tendril of tinsel, not a sprig of spruce. Dad kept his eyes firmly on the road ahead to avoid glimpsing an offensive outburst of fairy lights, or a smirking Santa in a shop window.

Ivy Cottage was miles down country lanes, then along a rutty track past a farm. The twins saw swelling hills and bare trees; they saw sheep, stiles and muddy paths. Dad stopped the car outside the farmhouse. The owner, Mrs Lamb, came out to give them the keys and show them the cottage. It stood in a ragged garden behind stone walls, with ivy scrambling over its porch. Inside was simple and old-fashioned but, Holly thought, rather cosy – or would be, when it was warmer. The floors had so many dips and rises that walking across them felt like being in a boat, and the stairs were narrow and twisty. The bedroom she was to share with Jonny had a window under the eaves, looking over the back garden.

Mrs Lamb, huddled in a fleece jacket, was explaining how to work the boiler.

'And you can have a log fire, if you like. There's plenty of logs outside, next to the stable – help yourself.'

'A log fire – lovely!' Mum said, rubbing her hands. 'Do you want to fetch some wood, twins, while I unpack?'

Holly's thoughts had fastened on the word *stable.* She thought for a wild moment there might be a pony in it, but the stable, at the end of an overgrown path, was empty. Still –

'There's no getting away from it, Dad!' she said, going back indoors with an armful of logs. 'We've got our very own stable!'

'Never mind that. Where's the TV?' Jonny asked.

'There isn't one,' Dad said.

Jonny's mouth fell open. 'You're kidding! No telly? How are we going to *survive*?'

'No self-respecting person,' Dad said firmly, 'needs television for entertainment, let alone survival. We're going to play Cluedo and Snakes and Ladders and Monopoly and draughts and dominoes. Traditional games. Now,' he added, 'no one is to mention *that word*, the C-word, for another two days. It – C – will begin on December the 24th at four o'clock. Not a moment before.'

Holly was the first person awake. She got out of bed and went to the window.

'There's a donkey in the garden!' she exclaimed.

'Yeah. Camels and three wise men as

well, I suppose.' Jonny could be grumpy in the mornings.

'No, there really *is* a donkey!' Holly crouched on the sill and rubbed at the glass. It was an amiable-looking donkey, grey, pale-muzzled, chewing at dried grass. Its ears twitched thoughtfully as it ate.

Mum and Holly dressed quickly and went out to introduce themselves. As the donkey seemed quite content, they left it grazing and went along to the farm to explain.

'Oh, sorry,' Mrs Lamb said. 'That's Balthasar. He lives there, usually, you see – it's his stable. I moved him down to the yard yesterday, but he must be a homing donkey. I'll fetch him back.'

'Can't he stay with us?' Holly said. 'I'll look after him. I'd like to, honest!'

Mrs Lamb looked at Mum; Mum nodded.

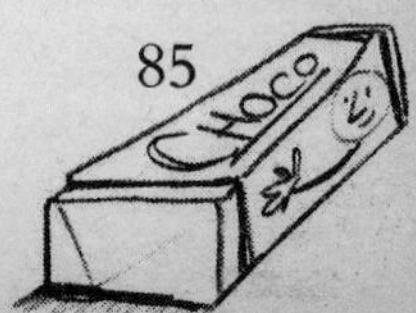

'Well, if you're sure. He'll be happier there. I'll fetch some hay and straw and feed, then, and show you what to do.'

Dad and Jonny were making toast when Holly burst into the kitchen a while later. 'We've got a *manger*!' she announced. 'A stable, a donkey and a manger!'

Dad gave her a Look from under his eyebrows.

'I didn't say it!' she protested. 'I didn't say the C-word! I'm just telling you what's out there!'

'What next?' Mum wondered.

'We're not doing badly,' Johnny said. He ticked off the items on his fingers. 'Holly, Ivy. Mrs Lamb – in a white fleece jacket! Stable, donkey and manger.'

'We've tried to Xscape,' Holly said, 'but X is coming after us, Dad.'

'Where's the gold, frankincense and myrrh coming from?' Jonny said, looking around, as if these gifts might be suspended from the ceiling.

'That's quite enough of that,' Dad snapped. 'Eat your breakfast. We're going on a walk. A long one.'

Later that evening, tired from their hill-walk and playing a fierce game of Ludo by the fire, they heard a scrabbling at the front door – a sound of strong claws on wood. They all heard it: scrabble, scrabble, whine.

'They don't have wolves in this part of the country, do they?' asked Jonny, making his eyes big.

'Don't be daft,' said Holly. 'It sounds like a dog. I'm going to see.'

'Be careful!' Mum was less confident with dogs than Holly was.

Even Holly stepped back when she opened the door and came face-to-face with an Alsatian. It *was* quite wolf-like; but

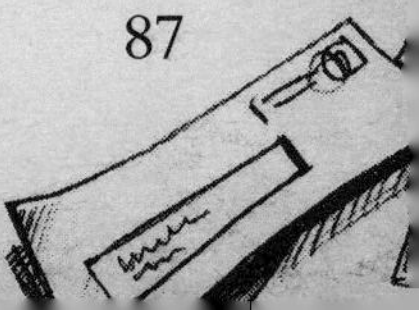

after they had exchanged wary glances, it sat on the doorstep, thumped its tail and gave her a pleading, hungry look. Taking pity, she let it in. It padded to the fire and lay down with a contented sigh, nose on paws. A gust of cold air came in with it. Holly shut the door hard, wondering if there might be snow. She thought of Balthasar, out in his stable, and hoped his thick coat would keep him warm. She shivered and went back to the Ludo, stepping over the dog.

'Are *all* the local waifs and strays going to invite themselves in?' Dad demanded.

'After this, I'll take it to the farmhouse and see if it belongs to Mrs Lamb,' Mum said, shaking the dice.

'There's one good thing,' said Dad. 'Unlike donkeys, stables and mangers, you don't get Alsatians at Chri –' He clapped a hand over his mouth.

Jonny's finger, thrusting across the Ludo board, almost poked Dad in the eye. 'You nearly said it! Nearly said the C-word! Wash your mouth out with soap and water!'

'Alsatian dogs,' Dad said, recovering from his mistake, 'don't figure in the mythology associated with this time of year.'

Jonny shook his head. 'You don't know much about dogs, do you, Dad?'

'What?'

'Alsatian,' Jonny said. 'German *Shepherd*.'

Mrs Lamb didn't recognise the dog, but said she would feed it and keep it overnight, and would phone the RSPCA and police next day.

'Well! What's the next ingredient?' said Mum.

They didn't have long to wait.

The next visitation to Ivy Cottage, on

the morning of Christmas Eve, was from three police officers. Everyone thought they had come about the dog, but that was only part of it.

'We're looking for a young boy,' one of the policemen explained. 'The dog you found was his. We think the dog, Beth, ran off while the boy – Chris, his name is, Chris Carpenter – was walking it near the village yesterday afternoon, and the boy went looking for her. Beth turned up here, but no sign of the lad. You haven't seen him, I suppose? Boy of seven, thin, brown hair, yellow anorak?'

'Poor thing, out in this weather!' exclaimed Mum. She made coffee for the policemen, while Jonny and Holly put on coats and wellies and gloves and went outside to search. They looked behind the holly tree, in the hollow where the stone wall dipped, and in the field beyond. No

sign of the boy. Nothing but a robin beady-eyeing them from a fence-post, and a taste of snow in the air.

They stood by the clock on the mantelpiece, dutifully waiting for four o'clock to strike. Dad checked his watch. Then, with the first *bong*:

'Ready, steady, *Christmas*!'

'Yessss!'

That was the signal for Jonny and Holly to dive into the larder for the Christmas tree, the box of decorations and the unopened cards. Dad, now that the official start had arrived, threw himself into it. He made hot punch with oranges and cinnamon, and stuck a sprig of holly in his hair. At last, Mum could put a tray of mince pies in the oven; the warm, spicy smell filled the cottage. Out came the paper angels Jonny and Holly had made

last year, the painted baubles, and the candle-holders. Out came Mum's table decoration of spruce and pine-cones, and the tree garlands. Soon the cottage was warm with candlelight.

'I keep thinking about that poor boy, Chris,' Mum said, with a half-eaten mince pie on her plate. 'Out in the cold. This doesn't seem right.'

'We've looked in all the nearby fields. So have the police,' Dad said. 'He'll turn up, I bet. Maybe he *has* turned up, by now.'

'There were three policemen,' Jonny said. 'Three wise men? Looking for a boy. They're bound to find him.'

'Following a star?' Holly said. 'No, following a dog called Beth. Bethlehem?'

'Don't be daft,' said Jonny. 'Who'd call a dog *Bethlehem*?'

'Someone might.' Holly pushed back the curtains and looked out of the window.

'Hey, it's snowing! Really snowing!'

Dad put another log on the fire. 'It's bleak midwinter all right.'

It snowed all evening. At bedtime, Holly looked out at the trees holding up their snow-laden branches, and at the cushiony snow that made her want to walk in it and make footprints. 'Deep and crisp and even,' she thought. Her breath misted the window; she rubbed it with her dressing-gown sleeve, and stared.

'Jonny! *Jonny*! There's a star, right over the stable!' It seemed to wink at her, brighter than all the others.

Grumbling, Jonny got out of bed and came to look.

'That's the Pole Star, dumbo. We're looking directly north, that's why it looks as if it's right over the stable. There's Plough, there's its pointers, and that's the Pole Star. It's always there. Not just on

Christmas Eve.'

But there must be more to it. All these coincidences couldn't be for nothing!

'I'm going there!' Holly said, fumbling for her slippers. 'Coming?'

'What, to the North Pole?'

'To the *stable*. Bring your torch.'

'What are you expecting?' Jonny complained, but he put on his slippers and dressing-gown. They crept down the twisty stairs. Mum and Dad sat in armchairs by the fire. Quickly, seeing the children, Mum stuffed something out of sight. Dad was a fraction slower; Holly glimpsed a red stocking and something silvery and shiny. Later on, when Mum and Dad crept upstairs with the stockings, she'd pretend to be soundly asleep. The grown-ups had to have their fun.

'I want to check that Balthasar's water isn't frozen,' she explained.

'What, at this time of night?' Mum glanced towards the window. 'In this snow?'

'We won't be a minute,' Holly pleaded. 'It's not every Christmas we get a real donkey to look after, is it?'

'Go on then. Put your coats and wellies on, and come straight back.'

It was so still and quiet that Holly knew there would be no more snow tonight. The sky was like a net of stars; as she looked she saw more and more of them, some cold and blue, others golden and nearer. Jonny shone his torch at a fresh set of footmarks leading to the stable door.

'Look!'

Holly held a finger to her lips as they crept the last few yards. Jonny shone the torch inside.

Balthasar was lying on the straw with his legs folded. Next to him, curled, snuggled against his warmth, was a small boy. Donkey and boy blinked in the torch-beam. The boy raised an arm to shield his eyes, but looked back at the twins quite calmly.

'It's you, isn't it! You're Chris!' Holly unbolted the door and crouched next to the boy. 'I knew you'd be here – all the signs *said* you must be! Don't worry about your dog, she's not lost any more. And now neither are you! You must be freezing, though!'

'Why didn't you come to the house?' Jonny asked.

Slowly, the boy got to his feet.

'Didn't think there'd be room,' he said. 'And I liked the look of the stable.' He stroked Balthasar's ears, and the donkey nuzzled him.

Mum's voice called from the back door: 'Holly! Jonny!'

'Come on,' Jonny urged. 'We've got soup

and mince pies and a warm fire. And a phone! You can phone your mum and dad and tell them you're safe. They must be out of their minds.'

'Mum and step-dad,' said the boy. 'Joe's not my real dad.'

Joe, Holly thought. Joe Carpenter. Right.

'And where *is* your real dad?' she asked, closing the stable door on the sleepy Balthasar. It wasn't a question to ask someone you'd only just met, but she couldn't help it. There was something about this boy. Who was he? He didn't seem afraid, though he had been wandering the hills for two nights at this darkest time of year. Maybe he had made a Great Xscape of his own, choosing his time to reappear.

'He's in Heaven,' said the boy.

Holly stared. Did he mean –?

Or did he mean –?

She looked closely at his head for any

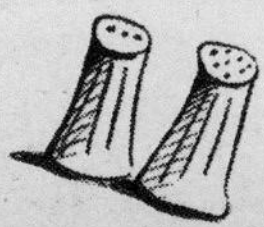

suggestion of a halo; she listened in case angel voices might suddenly ring out from the cottage roof; she checked that his boots really were making footprints in the snow. And, for a second, she thought the stars burned more brightly.

Would You Believe It?

Question:

What do you get when you cross a horse-backed ghost and a Dream Maker with a girl made of stone, too many baked beans, an invisible sister and a tiny figurine with needle-sharp fangs?

Answer:

You get a brilliant collection of stories about the allure of magic and mystery.

What's Cool About School

Question:

What do you get when you cross
a multi-coloured woollen worm,
a comical pencil and a hairless bear
with Aladdin's basket, a space-craft tree
and the world's biggest cucumber?

Answer:

You get a brilliant collection of stories
about the fun and the frights of school.

Give Me Some Space!

Question:

What do you get when you cross a disobedient broomstick and a special silver pig with a miraculous sunflower, a billion stars, a big black hole and a toaster that talks?

Answer:

You get a brilliant collection of stories about the marvels of space and science.